WICKED TEMPTATION

WICKED TEMPTATION

STARFIRE LAKE
BOOK THREE

VIVI PARISH

Editing by Rebecca Fairfax

Proofreading by Kristina Polacco

Cover Art by Naomi Lane

ISBN | Ebook: 979-8-9859408-4-8

ISBN | Paperback: 979-8-9859408-5-5

✾ Created with Vellum

For anyone who wishes they had a second chance to get things right.

CHAPTER 1

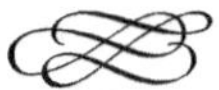

Rose did not want to call Jake Clark. The man she left her fiancé at the altar for, and the one who didn't even know she was still in love with him.

She glanced at the dog on her front seat. "At least you're safe now." Rose had seen the dog shivering under a tree and hadn't been able to leave her. It hadn't taken too much convincing to get the dog into the car.

The forecast had said the blizzard wouldn't hit for another few hours, but Mother Nature did what she wanted, the persnickety bitch. And the snow was coming down harder.

Rose's little car did not like the cold or snow, apparently. It wouldn't even start.

There was nobody else to call for help.

Not anymore.

Her parents were out of town for the long post-Thanksgiving weekend, and she wasn't about to ask one of her friends to send their guys out to help. Not in this weather.

The phone rang twice before a deep voice answered, hesitation evident. "Rose?"

"Jake? I'm sorry to bother you, but I didn't know who else to call." Rose had just seen him a little while ago at the grocery store, and though their conversation hadn't lasted long, it hadn't been as awkward as when she was still engaged to Henry.

"Are you okay?" Concern laced his voice, and Rose could almost picture his face—the furrow in his brow and the set of his jaw.

"I was trying to get this stray dog and my car won't start, and the local tow truck company is busy, my parents are out of town, and I don't know what to do."

"Tell me where you are."

She told him which shopping center to find her and ended the call. The black dog she'd found had curled up on the front passenger seat, still shivering. Both of them were soaked from the rain and snow.

Strong winds whipped through the trees, and Rose tried not to worry as the car shifted from side to side.

The dog glanced around in alarm, settling her gaze on Rose. "It's okay, sweetie. What should I call you? Do you have a name already?" A head tilt was the only reply. Rose reached her hand out again for the pup to sniff. "How do you like the name Daisy?"

There was no collar on the dog, and Rose was worried someone had dumped her.

A kiss on the fingers. "Daisy it is."

Barely ten minutes later, Jake's truck appeared ahead. Rose could have cried in relief.

"We're rescued, little one. Today really is your lucky day."

The dog looked up at Rose as if to say, 'I know.' Those big brown eyes were full of hope, but Rose could see a tinge of fear that made her heart break. She let the dog sniff her hand again and then rubbed her ears. "You're a sweet, good girl." The words earned her a tail thump. "Should we let the sexy man take us home?" Another thump. "Come on, let's get out of this mess, what do you think?"

Jake hopped out of his truck with something in his hand, and a golf umbrella open. He handed Rose a lead that she slipped around Daisy's neck without issue. Jake held the umbrella overhead as he escorted Rose and her new friend to his truck.

Rose hesitated before she got in. "We're going to get your seats wet."

"Don't worry about it, they've had wet dogs on them before." He smiled at her, and Rose's heart almost stopped.

Damn his green eyes. She'd always been weak for that shade of deep green, the canopy of leaves in a forest.

Once they were all in and on the road, Jake spoke first. "I'm sorry I don't have towels or anything for you. I was already on the road and didn't want to make you wait any longer than you had to. I called Randy down at the shop and they'll be out here to tow your car when they can."

"You didn't have to do that. I kept trying to get through to the shop and nobody answered."

"Ah," he held up a finger in a triumphant gesture. "I have Randy's cell."

"That explains it. You've got connections."

Jake shrugged. "It's all about who you know." The truck hit an ice patch and slid a few feet to the right, narrowly missing a hanging limb and catching Rose off guard. She managed not to scream but couldn't stop the gasp and clutched the center console in a death grip.

Jake got the truck straightened out and back on the road. He covered her hand with his. The warmth and strength that emanated from him helped Rose relax - ever so slightly.

"I've got you, Rose. I won't let anything happen. You're safe with me, remember?"

She remembered, possibly too well.

A memory of Jake driving them around town in the middle of the night, the town quiet and deserted, popped up. They had gone to see a movie and then spent time in the backseat of his truck in a dark corner of the parking lot.

Rose's phone dinged and brought her out of her memory. A message from her friend and temporary landlord, Stacey, said their house lost power. Rose had moved into the studio apartment above their garage. If the main house didn't have power, neither did her apartment. "Crap."

"What happened?" Jake's hand went back on the steering wheel, and Rose tried not to miss his touch. It had been so long since she'd felt as safe as she did with him.

Rose didn't want to burden him any more than she already had today. "The power is out at my place. I'm sure it'll be on again soon, though." She glanced out the window at the falling snow. The road was rapidly disappearing beneath a blanket of white. The truck slowed to almost a crawl, Jake maneuvering it expertly through the weather.

Jake shook his head. "I don't feel comfortable taking you home to a dark house. Not in a blizzard like this."

"I guess you could take me to my parent's house, but…" She wasn't fully convinced about the idea even as she spoke it.

"It's on the other side of town, up a massive hill." Jake wasn't wrong about that. She'd had difficulty traversing that hill many times.

He didn't take his eyes off the road. "I'm going to suggest something, and you can't get mad, but you have to say yes." *Bossy as ever.*

"I don't like the sound of that."

"Stay with me." Jake must have anticipated her reaction because he held up a hand as he said. "Just until the storm is over, and your power is back on."

Rose's heart almost stopped. She couldn't deny that the opportunity to spend time with him was appealing, and the electricity running through her body meant she was definitely still attracted to him. But they'd hardly spoken in years except for the odd run-ins in town, and even those had been few and far between once she'd moved to college and then in with Henry at his apartment on the north shore.

She hadn't worked up the nerve to reach out since she called off her wedding almost six months ago. The wedding that she called off because she was still in love with him.

If she hadn't just seen him at the grocery store earlier, she probably wouldn't have thought to call him for help. "I don't know if that's a good idea. I'm sure the power will be back on soon enough."

She checked on Daisy in the back. She was upright and looked as though she were trying to be as small as possible against the back of the leather seats. Rose knew she couldn't bring Daisy to an apartment without heat and didn't want to risk Jake not taking her in.

"Rose, I'm not taking you back to a dark house with no heat during a blizzard. My house isn't far, and I promise Randy will get your car safely to his shop. I'll take you home as soon as your power is back, and the roads are safe." Jake spared a second from watching the road to wink at her, a grin on his face.

Her resolve melted.

It was nice to be rescued. That hadn't happened in a long, long time.

"Okay, but just for tonight."

"We'll see."

CHAPTER 2

The walk up to the small porch and front door was more harrowing than Rose cared to admit, especially since the dog kept trying to jump in the snow and bite at it. Rose couldn't help but laugh at the sight.

Rose struggled to hold the lead Jake had put on the dog and slipped on a patch of ice. The ground went out from underneath her, and the sky filled her vision as she tumbled backwards.

Jake's strong arms caught her before she hit the ground. "Easy there." Jake's breath tickled her ear as he steadied her, his chest against her back. It took every ounce of her willpower not to sink into his warmth.

She forced herself to take a step away.

"Thanks," she turned as she spoke. Her gaze met his, and for a split second the world narrowed to the two of them - standing on the walkway with snow falling in furious swirls around them, their breath mingling in the cold. She couldn't remember what started the fight that led to their break up after high school, and regret filled her again.

Jake broke their connection first when he looked behind her and called the dog back to them. "Daisy! Hey pretty girl, come here!" Rose pretended not to notice the way her heart kicked up a notch at Jake's use of 'pretty girl.'

The dog bounded for him and followed him up the porch steps and inside the house. So much for nervous and scared. It was as if Daisy thought she was already home.

Rose followed carefully and tried not to melt at the adorableness of Jake loving on the dog, rubbing her ears and wiggly butt. He'd always had a soft spot for animals, dogs especially.

She had no idea how the next few hours were going to go. They hadn't spent any amount of time together since that awful summer before college. The occasional awkward run in at a store or on the street were the only times they'd seen each other.

Nerves bubbled in her stomach. She'd chickened out every time she'd lifted the phone to reach out to him over the last few months.

Rose had wanted to spend time with him, and now she had an unknown amount of it, thanks to the blizzard and a power outage. When the Universe listened, it over-delivered.

"Welcome to Casa Jake."

Warmth enveloped her as she crossed the threshold, and Jake closed the door behind her.

He helped peel the jacket down her arms, and stepped away so she could undo the laces of her boots and step out of them.

"I'm going to get this girl settled in the spare crate in my room. Make yourself at home."

Rose bent down and let Daisy come to her for some scratches under her neck. "Who's a good girl? You are, yes you are, sweetie."

Jake's leg brushed against hers as he bent down and waited for Daisy to approach him. The dog eagerly went from standing in front of Rose to wiggling between them both and getting as much love as she could.

Jake stood slowly. "Okay, let's go Daisy. I have a nice cozy bed in a safe crate with some yummy treats and water. How does that sound?"

Daisy's tongue lolled out of her mouth and her tail whipped the air behind her.

"I think that's a yes," Rose laughed. She watched the two of them as they disappeared down the hall and into a doorway. Jake had grown out of his gangly teenage self and filled out his frame. It was hard *not* to stare.

Alone for a few minutes, Rose gingerly stepped into the home Jake had made for himself. It was quintessential Jake: earthy colors on the walls, comfort and utility blended into one.

The entry opened into a cozy living space with a mounted flatscreen, large couch, and photos on the walls and the mantle. There was a kitchen off to the right, a hall that led further into the back of the house, and a small staircase that disappeared around a corner to a second level.

"Your house is lovely," she called out. Unsure what to do with herself, she stood awkwardly in the space between the entry and the house.

Jake reappeared a few seconds later. "Thanks," he said. "Come on in. Let's get you out of those wet clothes."

She sputtered. "What?"

He winked and her entire body warmed. "I mean we can put your wet clothes in the wash and dryer if you'd like. And you can borrow something of mine."

Wear Jake's clothes? Why not just offer to knock her out while he's at it?

"Oh, um, sure. Dry clothes would be nice."

"One sec." He disappeared back into the doorway as before. Rose could hear something bang, and a curse.

"Everything okay?"

"Yeah, yeah, fine." His voice was muffled, but he reappeared a minute later with a bundle of clothes in his hands. "The duffel bag on the shelf decided it didn't like me, that's all. I grabbed a few different options for you."

She took the offered items, grateful to be able to get out of the wet leggings and shirt she still wore. "Thanks. Bathroom?"

"Door on the left," he said as he pointed down the same hall.

"I'll just be a minute."

"No rush. I'll make us some hot chocolate. Make yourself at home." Jake disappeared into the kitchen. Rose followed his directions to the small bathroom in the hall.

She caved to the temptation to pull his flannel shirt to her nose and breathe in his scent. Cedarwood and cologne.

Rose peeled off the cold, wet clothes and pulled on the too-big sweats and shirt from Jake. She took a moment and held the flannel tight around herself and imagined it was his arms.

What was she even doing here? In his house, and wearing his clothes? It was barely hours ago that she'd still been too afraid to call him and ask him for coffee or something to catch up.

The washer and dryer were stacked in a small alcove of the bathroom. Rose put them in for a quick dry cycle and hit the "start" button.

The lights went out.

"Shit." She scrambled to find her phone in the dark. She heard it hit the floor, but it didn't illuminate on impact.

"You okay, Rose?" Jake's footsteps were clear in the complete absence of sound.

"Yeah, sorry. I didn't mean to – ouch." She'd gotten herself turned around and walked into the door. Or a wall.

"I don't think the power going out during a blizzard is something you can really take credit for."

Rose heard the door open, and then there was a bit of light shining into the room. Rose had walked into the wall next to the door. "It went off after I turned on the dryer." She saw her phone on the floor, grabbed it, and stepped into the hall with Jake.

"Ah, okay. Should be a simple fix. Come on, I'll show you to the couch – or kitchen if you want."

"Couch is good." She followed him to the front of the house and tried not to humiliate herself even more by tripping on a rug or table or something.

"Here you go." Jake shone the flashlight from his phone to light up the living room and couch. "I'll be right back."

Rose sat on the couch and waited as he disappeared. The darkness and silence in an unfamiliar house was eerie enough to make Rose keep checking her phone. There wasn't much battery left, so she only used it to track the time since Jake had left. She sent a quick message to her cousin Megan about where she was for the night.

Rose wanted to tell her sister, Rebecca, but didn't want to deal with answering a million questions. Megan would keep the information to herself and would compile a list of questions to interrogate Rose with later.

After what felt like ages but was less than ten minutes, the lights came on again. Rose heard the heat click on and let out a sigh of relief.

Jake reappeared. "Not sure why it happened but a fuse blew." Jake smiled as he braced his arms against the back of the couch. "Do you still want hot chocolate?"

"Oh, only if you want some. I don't want you to go to even more trouble. Especially since I blew a fuse and maybe broke your dryer."

Jake shrugged. "It's under warranty. I'll make the drinks." He disappeared into the kitchen. Though Rose couldn't see him from her corner spot, the echoes of cabinet doors closing and a drawer or two sliding reached her.

Rose tried not to stare as Jake carried in a tray that held two steaming mugs, a bag of large marshmallows, and an assortment of sugar cookies in multiple winter-themed shapes.

"Are those your mom's famous cookies?" Rose accepted the mug he offered and let the heat seep into her still-chilled fingers.

"Her recipe, but I made them." Jake sat near her on the couch, but not too close.

Rose took a snowman cookie that had red, green, and gold sprinkles baked into it. "This is adorable." The initial crunch followed by softness as she bit into it was perfect. "Mm, and so good! You made them?"

"Don't sound so surprised. Mom taught me a few years ago. Said it was so I'd stop bothering her every week."

Rose finished off the cookie in another two bites and reached for another. She decided to test the water, to see if there was even a reason for her to be nervous – or for her to gather her courage and confess her feelings for Jake.

"Your girlfriend must love them. She's lucky." She took a sip of her drink and failed at not being obvious.

Jake only grinned at her, a curious expression on his face.

"What?" Rose asked.

"Nothing. No girlfriend."

"Oh. Your wife, then?"

Jake shook his head. "Not married. Just me, and whatever dog I'm fostering."

Rose nodded. It was unfathomable to her that he could still be single. She'd hoped, of course, but to find out he was indeed available made her heart skip a few beats.

How could this man – ruggedly handsome, clearly successful, thoughtful, kind, funny man be unattached?

"Now you're wondering why I'm single." He grabbed a cookie from the tray and sat against the back of the couch.

"No, I'm not. I'm – okay, maybe. But it's none of my business."

"There's a simple answer, if you want to ask the question."

A challenge. "If I had to guess, I'd say it's because you've had a recent heartbreak and aren't ready to try again. Am I close?"

A light in his eyes dimmed a bit. "Not a recent one, no." He looked away for a moment. "Is that why you're single?"

"How do you know that I am?"

Jake raised an eyebrow at her, as if he couldn't believe she asked that question. "You're not wearing your engagement ring. Plus, it's hard to miss the talk about how Rose Keating left her debonair fiancé at the altar. Runaway bride, jilted groom – not gossip that happens a lot in Starfire Lake."

Rose looked down at her mug. The steam had faded, and the marshmallows were more like white puddles in the chocolate. "Yeah, well. It'd be nice if the gossip would end."

"He wasn't a good guy?" Jake's voice was soft.

"Henry? No, he was. That's what makes the rest of it so hard. People understand when you end a relationship with an asshole. It's obvious and easy for them to swallow and move on. But when it looks like your relationship is perfect, people have difficulty with it ending – especially when you leave Prince Charming standing in a church." She put the mug on the end table next to her, careful to set it on the coaster.

"You were never really a fan of Prince Charming, if I remember."

Rose met Jake's gaze. "No, I wasn't," she whispered.

"Too boring," he said. His gaze dropped to her mouth and then back up to meet her eyes.

Her heart pounded against her ribs. "Yes. Too boring."

"You need adventure. More of a Robin Hood fan." Jake's voice had gotten quieter.

"Who wouldn't love a guy who helps those who need it?"

His eyes widened at her use of the word 'love.' "Rose," Jake breathed. He stood, put his mug on the tray, and sat next to her, his thigh against hers. He turned to face her, and Rose could barely breathe for the closeness of him.

"Hmm?" She wasn't sure the sound was intentional.

Jake brushed a stray hair from her forehead. "Why haven't you called me?"

"I did," she confessed.

He shook his head. "Not today. I mean after you left him. It's been months – is there someone else?"

"No, I did call you. Well, I tried. I kept hanging up before I could hit the 'call' button."

"There's nobody else?" That was hope in his eyes.

Rose shook her head. "No."

"Why didn't you marry him?"

Rose stared at Jake, the reason himself. But she couldn't admit to the whole truth. Not yet. "Henry was a good boyfriend and would have been a good husband. But I didn't love him enough, and I didn't realize it until it was almost too late."

"Almost."

She nodded. "I just…couldn't do it." Rose watched a battle she didn't understand happen on Jake's face. "You never answered my question."

"Why I'm single."

"Yes," she breathed.

"I haven't found anyone who compares."

"To what?"

Jake brushed his knuckles along her cheek. "You."

CHAPTER 3

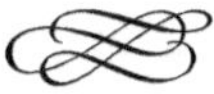

Rose almost laughed. Almost. The look in his eyes stopped her. Jake was serious. "That's – what?"

"You asked why I'm still single. That's my answer."

Her instinct to run, to move, warred against her desire to kiss him. The need to run, to put space between her and Jake was strong. That's what she did when things were too much, too overwhelming. She needed space. But the other part of herself wanted him. Wanted him to kiss her, to touch her, to keep her still.

The moment he looked like he might do exactly that, Rose jumped up. Adrenaline coursed through every piece of her body.

"I need – I..."

"You can walk laps around the coffee table if you need to."

She whirled to face him. Jake hadn't moved a muscle. "What?"

"You need to move, right?"

"Don't mock me." Rose was tired of people making fun of her, and her tone was sharp. All she could hear was 'runaway bride.'

Jake held up his hands. "I'm not mocking you, Rose. It helps you process if you're moving. You've always needed to walk it out. I'm offering a solution, so you don't go running into the blizzard."

"Oh," was the only thing she could say. Jake was the first person, aside from Megan, who noticed her need for movement to help her brain. "You don't care if I just walk for a few minutes?"

"Not even a little bit. Would you like me to get you some water?"

She nodded. "Please." Rose waited for Jake to stand and go to the kitchen before she wiped at the tears that sprung up.

Then she walked. At first around the coffee table a few times. Then down the hall. She didn't understand his confession. Or why he would admit to it so damn quickly. It hadn't been that long since he saved her from the side of the road, and it had been years since they'd had a real conversation.

Of course, the best thing to do would be to ask for more information. What did he mean nobody compared to her? What qualities was he measuring?

Did he expect her to be the same girl she was when they were teenagers? How disappointed would he be when he discovered she wasn't?

On one pass, Jake simply handed her a glass of water as she went by and went to sit on the couch.

Rose took a sip and kept her loop.

Up and down the hall. Front door, turn, up the hall. Back wall, spin, down the hall.

Again and again.

Until she heard Daisy moving in the crate. Rose cracked the door open and saw Daisy with her tail wagging. "Hey, pretty girl. You feeling okay?" The water bowl looked almost empty, and the other bowl had been licked clean. "Ready to come out?"

The dog pawed at the door of the crate. Rose laughed and stepped into the room. She bent down and let Daisy sniff her fingers first, and then opened the lock and swung the door open.

Daisy immediately tackled Rose and knocked her on her back, and kissed any part of Rose she could.

Rose sputtered and giggled and tried to pet the wiggling dog. "Oh, okay. Yes, I love you, too. Yes, I know. Oh, okay."

Daisy disappeared, and Rose tilted her head to see Jake. He'd squatted in the doorway and Daisy was on her back, wiggling for belly rubs.

"Sorry. I should have asked before I let her out. She was just too cute." Rose sat up and brushed herself off and wiped at the stray Daisy hairs.

"Did you hit Rose with the puppy eyes? Oh, yeah?"

It took Rose an extra second to realize the higher pitch of Jake's voice was aimed at Daisy. She stared at the way he adjusted his entire body to make sure Daisy didn't feel threatened; his broad shoulders scrunched in an unthreatening way, his voice gentle and soft and just for the dog at his feet. Rose melted.

She could see the look of love in Daisy's eyes. That dog was a goner, and it was likely that Jake was, too.

"I think she might need to go outside. I can take her." Rose stood and started to leave the room. That's when she noticed the room had a massive bed against the far wall. And a dresser across from it, next to the door to the hall. And a closet in the corner, door propped open, and a duffle bag crumpled on the floor.

Not a spare room.

Jake's bedroom.

Jake stood. "That's okay. I'll take her so you don't have to go out in the cold again. We won't be long." Jake smiled at Rose, glanced behind her in the direction of his bed, and then back at her. Her entire body heated under his gaze. "Come on, pretty girl."

Rose went to take a step when Daisy leapt up and trotted behind Jake.

The dog. 'Pretty girl' was the dog.

Rose needed to get a grip. She followed Jake and Daisy down the hall and then waited on the couch for them to come back in.

It didn't take long before Daisy bounded back into the room and jumped on the couch next to Rose.

"Feel better?" Rose gave Daisy some ear rubs and then belly rubs when the dog flopped onto her back, paws up. Daisy sat up, gave Rose a bunch of kisses, and zoomed around the couch a few times before she ran out of the room. "Okay, bye wild girl!"

Rose was still trying to sort out her reaction to Jake's confession by the time Jake and Daisy came back in. Daisy claimed the spot next to Rose and curled up, finally worn out. Jake took a seat on the opposite side of the L-shape.

"I'm not sure the blizzard is going to slow down any time soon. We can't do much else other than hunker down, but we can put a movie on, and I can whip up a quick dinner if you're hungry."

It was past the time Rose usually ate but she'd been too distracted by the blizzard, getting stranded and then rescued, and by Jake to notice.

"Food sounds good. But I insist on helping somehow."

"Okay, if you insist," Jake laughed. "I have some lasagna left-overs we can heat up."

Rose followed Jake into the kitchen, and waited at the entryway as he got things together. His movements were intentional and confident as he got their late dinner ready. She'd seen her uncles spend five minutes looking for something they use every day in their own kitchens in their houses that they'd lived in for decades. None of them moved around their kitchens with the level of surety that Jake moved in his.

Jake lived alone, and that could account for his familiarity with his own home. But not everyone who lived alone was comfortable cooking for themselves. She was fairly adept in the kitchen but didn't move with the same surety that Jake had.

"How can I help?"

"Uh, depends. Do you want to eat in here at the table or in the living room?"

The sound of her mother and Henry's mother clutching their figurative pearls at the idea of eating somewhere other than a dining table echoed in Rose's head. "I don't have a preference."

"If we eat in the living room, we can watch the weather or a movie."

Rose recognized the offer of a buffer. "Living room it is."

Jake smiled. "I have folding trays against the entertainment center under the tv. You can pick our spots. I don't have a favorite."

Rose found the tables and got them set up, and Jake brought the plates of food.

"That smells amazing. Did you make it?" Rose's mouth watered as she eyed the slice of noodles, meat sauce, and cheese on the table in front of her.

"Not this time. This is from Mom. She loaded me up when I was over there a couple of days ago to check on the house ahead of the storm."

Rose knew it would be delicious. Mrs. Clark had fed Rose a lot over the course of the two years Rose and Jake had been together as teenagers. She tried not to worry what Mrs. Clark might think of her now. Much as the older woman had been kind and welcoming to Rose as a teenager, Rose was sure Mrs. Clark's opinion of her had changed after the breakup, and probably again more recently still with all of the 'runaway bride' gossip that had spread.

"Weather or a movie?"

Rose glanced at Jake and found his gaze fixed on her. He'd always been able to read her mood better than anyone. "Weather check and then a movie, I think."

"Good deal." He pulled up the right channel. The forecast for the night and next day were "blizzard, and more blizzard." The storm had decided to sit right on top of Long Island, a rare occurrence, even in December.

It was unlikely that Rose would get home any time soon, and she was even more grateful she'd packed an emergency backpack for her car. And even happier she'd remembered to grab it when Jake saved her and Daisy.

Her hand froze in midair, fork and all. The bag she'd packed was still in the backseat of Jake's truck. There was no actual reason for her to have borrowed his clothes.

"Everything okay?"

Her cheeks burned. "Yeah. Just remembering that I have a bag with my own clothes in the back of your truck."

Jake stared at Rose, silent for a beat and then laughed. "Is that what's in that bag? I brought it in for you before. It's by the front door."

"Really?" Rose whipped her head around to look. Sure enough, tucked against the wall next to the door was her blue emergency backpack. "I feel like an idiot. I walked right by it half a dozen times before!" She sighed.

"It's been a stressful day. Don't beat yourself up."

"I'll change after we eat and give your clothes back." She took another bite and tried not to look as embarrassed as she felt.

"No, you won't."

Rose glanced up at the command in his voice. "What?"

"There's no reason to change unless my clothes are uncomfortable."

"Oh, no. They're, um…" Rose's body heated under his gaze. "They're very comfortable." She clenched her thighs together when he growled.

"Good. Then no reason for you to change right away. Any requests for a movie?"

Rose shook her head and took another bite. She wasn't normally one to follow orders, but Rose almost squeaked out a 'yes, sir,' at his tone. Jake hadn't been all that dominant when they were together in high school. Apparently, he'd grown into more than just his physical frame.

When had *that* happened?

Jake picked an older movie, one he knew she'd already seen. "Something familiar," was all he said about his choice.

They finished their food in easy quiet, though Rose had to force her eyes from Jake to the tv more than once. He either didn't notice or pretended not to see her watch him from her perch across from him.

She helped him clean up when they were both finished. Jake gave Daisy a little more food and took her outside again. Rose watched from the back door, arms crossed against the cold air that seeped in. Daisy was definitely a fan of snow. Jake tossed small handfuls into the air, and Daisy jumped and snapped at them, and at the flakes that still fell from the dark sky.

Rose's heart swelled. Whatever happened between her and Jake, Daisy was safe and would be loved, even if she ended up in a different forever home. The thought made Rose's heart ache. Daisy and Jake looked like they belonged together. But who was Rose to put that expectation on Jake after spending only a handful of hours together? If Rose thought Daisy would be at all happy in the small above-garage apartment, Rose would keep her. But it wouldn't be fair to take Daisy away from a yard, and Jake.

Rose gave them space as Jake and Daisy came back into the warmth of the house. Rose snagged Daisy before she could run away and wrapped her in the towel Jake left by the back door. She dried off all four paws and rubbed along Daisy's belly to get the snow off. Daisy wiggled and foot stomped the entire time. Rose let go and Daisy wiggled away, likely in search of somewhere comfortable and warm.

Jake started to peel off the layers of winter gear. The area by the back door was small, so Rose backed into the kitchen to give him space. Jake lifted the sweatshirt over his head, and Rose caught a glimpse of bare skin and the top of his jeans.

Her body's reaction to that slip of skin was akin to looking at a feast while starving. Except she didn't want food. Oh no. That wasn't the appetite that roared to life in her belly.

Jake dropped the sweatshirt onto the pile by the door and stepped out of the boots. Rose caught every fluid move and memorized it.

She backed up more as he walked into the kitchen. He locked his gaze on hers, and Rose saw the desire in his green eyes. It mirrored her own. He walked her backwards until she bumped into the counter. "Oh."

Jake stepped so close that her breasts brushed against his chest. He dipped his head until his lips touched her ear. Rose tried not to whimper. "See something you like?"

She went weak at the knees. "Um." She couldn't exactly lie because he'd caught her mid-stare-and drool.

Jake chuckled. The sound reverberated through Rose. He pulled away and filled a glass with water. She watched as he drank his fill, the glass lifted against his mouth. Two drops escaped his lips and trailed down his throat as it worked. Rose had to pin her hands behind her to stop herself from reaching for those two little beads of water.

Jake filled another glass of water and left it on the counter next to her. "In case you need a drink, too."

Rose grabbed Jake by his shirt before he could leave and pulled him close. His mouth crashed against hers, and nothing would be the same ever again.

Rose's world had been off kilter for years. But the moment Jake's lips had touched hers, it shifted back into place.

Jake wrapped his arms around her waist and held her against him, as if he were afraid that she'd disappear. Rose wound her arms around his neck and leaned into the kiss. She trailed her nails up the back of his neck and buried her fingers in his hair.

Jake growled and lifted her onto the counter. Rose wrapped her legs around him and pressed herself against him everywhere she could.

Jake pulled away and took a few gulping breaths. "We should – not stop exactly, but slow down." He relinquished his hold on her and stepped back. She let him.

Why? She wanted to ask but words were beyond her. Lips swollen, she could only nod. He brushed a few loose strands of hair out of her face. Rose couldn't read his expression, but she'd noticed the hardness of his cock through his jeans a few moments ago.

Jake helped her down off the counter and handed her the glass of water. "In case you're thirsty." He kissed her forehead and left before she could stop him a second time.

She was in trouble. But Rose wasn't sure that was a problem.

CHAPTER 4

The rest of the movie passed in a blur. Rose couldn't focus on anything except the lingering feeling of Jake's lips against hers, the strength of his arms around her. She tried to watch the movie instead of him, but her gaze drifted over to him more than once.

Jake was stretched out from the corner of the L-shape of the couch, his legs out in front of him. Daisy curled up next to his feet, head on his leg. Jake tucked an arm behind his head, which caused his shirt to ride up a bit and that same bit of bare skin was visible again. Rose spent half the movie focused on that tantalizing spot of Jake's body. The other half of the movie she spent in a daydream about the kiss they shared in the kitchen.

Rose's body remembered his touch. Oh yes, the moment his lips covered hers, her body woke up and wanted more. Memories of them tangled together and exploring each other would not leave Rose alone. They'd been each other's first everything and had spent hours together learning what gave the other pleasure.

She'd never shared such an intense physical connection with anyone else, and nobody else had shown such a dedicated focus on her body and her pleasure.

Rose startled as the movie ended and Jake stood. He called Daisy to go outside again.

"One more time, pretty girl." He patted her belly and nudged her to get up. Rose struggled not to laugh at Daisy's complete reluctance to move.

Jake turned his gaze on Rose. "Glad you're enjoying the show."

Rose stretched her legs out and grinned. "Oh, I'm enjoying quite a bit tonight."

Jake's eyes darkened, and his grin turned wicked. Heat trailed through Rose's body and settled low in her belly.

Jake put one arm on the arm of the couch and leaned down. He nuzzled his face against her hair but pulled back. "Just wait till I get back inside." His voice was low and gruff, and Rose couldn't come up with a response.

Daisy chose that moment to hop off the couch and trudge after Jake.

Rose didn't want to wait, but she also didn't want to get caught up in the physical attraction that clearly had not dissipated with time. If anything, Rose wanted him more now, to feel his body moving with hers, to explore each other as adults rather than awkward almost-twenty-year-olds.

For the first time since before she was with Henry, Rose *wanted*. For years, she'd written off the level of attraction she shared with Jake as a fluke of first love. She convinced herself it wouldn't have lasted even if she and Jake had stayed together.

Denial was a powerful mindfuck, if ever there was one.

Still, caution and taking things slow would be the wiser choice. Jake may not want the same things out of life, and there was no better person in town more qualified than Rose to understand the importance of shared goals, values, and attraction.

A few minutes later, Daisy bounded in and jumped on the opposite side of the couch, stretching herself across three cushions. "Making yourself at home already, huh?"

Daisy let out a huff but didn't move.

"It's a good thing you're sweet, Daisy, or I think taking up that much space was punishment for making you go outside in the snow again." Jake came around the couch into view.

Rose saw the opportunity and before she could second-guess herself, said, "You could sit here next to me, keep me warm during the next movie. As long as you don't bite."

It was an effort to keep her breathing steady with Jake so close as he lowered himself to the spot next to her.

"I only bite when asked, as I'm sure you remember." He draped his arm across the back of the couch behind her.

Rose remembered. One summer she'd had to find a swimsuit with a skirt bottom and wear longer sundresses because of the hickeys Jake enjoyed leaving at the tops of her inner thighs. *"You're mine and I'm yours, and these are secret reminders that I've claimed you, Rose."*

She burned at the memory and ached to have him between her legs again, to have another secret mark of his claim on her instead of the invisible one on her heart.

The idea of it was ludicrous of course. Earlier in the kitchen was an anomaly, a moment of weakness for both of them. A moment of physical attraction didn't mean there would be room for more, even if Rose wanted it.

Jake chose a movie that Rose once again couldn't focus on, not with him playing with her hair. It was such a soft moment that Rose wondered if he remembered how much she loved for someone to brush and play with her hair.

But the excitement of the day caught up to her and it was difficult to keep her eyes open. Rose nodded off once or twice before Jake pulled her against him, and in the hazy spot right before she fell asleep Rose could have sworn Jake whispered something that sounded like "I want to keep you."

CHAPTER 5

Jake's warmth wrapped around Rose, more comforting than any blanket. It had been so long since she'd felt anywhere close to this content and she didn't want to give it up. But she didn't know how to keep it, either.

They'd been so young when they first dated, and when things got confusing and difficult, Jake walked away. Then she'd met Henry and almost married him - she was the one to walk away that time. It wasn't as though there were many instances where she could say that yes, she stuck it out and knew with complete certainty that she knew how to make a relationship last through trials and hardship.

Jake stirred against her, Rose scrunched her shoulders and giggled at the feeling of his face buried against her neck. He growled, a low, possessive sound that rumbled against her bare skin and made her body react in ways she'd forgotten it could; his arm tightened around her waist, and he rolled her onto her back underneath him.

"Did I wake you?" Rose was almost breathless, and all he'd done was breathe and roll her over. She was in so deep with him that she didn't think she'd ever need to come up for air.

"Mm, no. I haven't fallen asleep yet." Jake punctuated his sentences with kisses on her neck. "My brain is too busy."

"Yours, too?"

Jake stopped his adoration of her neck and lifted himself to look at her. Concern marred his features, but his voice was soft as he asked, "Do you want to talk about it?"

Rose knew he'd let it go if she said no, but the truth was that she did want to talk. She needed to process everything in her head and the second-best way she knew how to do that was out loud, usually to someone else. She sure as hell didn't want to leave his arms to go walk laps again.

"If you don't mind listening to me ramble a bunch of nonsense until something clicks in my head."

"I'd love to listen to you ramble." Jake pulled away just enough to give her space to breathe. She adjusted herself to lean into him but stared up at the ceiling.

Rose was quiet, not sure how to explain the jumble in her head.

"Would it help if we had something to eat?"

"It's like two in the morning."

"So? Grilled cheese is easy and delicious. Want some?"

Her stomach growled. "I guess so," she laughed.

"Let's go." Jake helped Rose untangle from the blanket they'd been under and led the way to the kitchen. "Have a seat," he gestured to the table.

Rose padded to the little round table and took a chair. She watched Jake as he expertly maneuvered around the kitchen and fired up the stove for their sandwiches. It was a few minutes before she gathered the courage to say anything.

"I think I'm scared." Rose stared at her hands and let the confession hang in the space. Jake didn't say anything, his silence as he worked an encouragement for her to continue when she's ready.

"My life has been such a mess for a long time, and I don't

know how to move through it. I feel stuck, and I have for a long time. While I was with … him, I thought I was happy enough. But is that really a thing? And I dreaded the wedding. I never imagined a big wedding, even as a teenager, so when it morphed from family and close friends into what felt like a modern attempt at a society wedding…"

Tears welled and Rose brushed them away with a hand.

"I couldn't breathe. I kept telling myself that he was a great guy - and he is, really. He's kind, sweet, and smart. But I could not figure out why I dreaded the wedding. That week of bonding at the family house was hell. I kept it hidden though - nobody knew how I really felt."

Rose hadn't wanted to think about that week, or the almost-wedding, since it happened. Henry, for all that he was the wrong man for her, had been confused and frustrated but never once had he blamed or yelled at her or shown any sign of anger.

Henry's mother, however, had been a force to reckon with, blaming Rose for ruining Henry's life and accusing her of all manner of awful things. Henry had apologized for his mother's behavior as his father had pulled the screaming woman out of the living room of their previously-shared apartment.

"But it wasn't until Megan asked me how I knew Henry was The One that I couldn't hide from myself anymore. I managed to come up with some lame answer, but the question woke me up. I spent the night before my almost-wedding rethinking every decision I'd made and wondering where I went wrong."

Rose dared a glance at Jake. He was almost done with the sandwiches. He slid them onto plates, turned off the stove, and brought them to the table. He set the plates down and sat across from her.

"Did you figure it out?" His voice was soft, and Rose detected worry.

"The only thing I decided that night was that I couldn't marry

Henry. But I didn't know how to not go through with it. Megan helped."

Jake's words were gruff as he finished a bite. "Thank God for Megan."

"What do you mean?"

"If she hadn't helped, would you have married him?"

"I don't know." It was the truth. She took a bite of her sandwich. "This is delicious." She focused on finishing it, and Jake did the same with his.

He only spoke again after they'd eaten every last bite, and he took the plates to the sink. "I'm thankful as fuck Megan helped because it led you back to me. To being here, with me. And I will get down on my knees to any deity and thank them every day."

"Oh. I…" Rose had hoped Jake felt something for her, especially after he'd confessed to still having feelings, but it was hard for her to get her hopes up. She needed certainty after everything she'd been through, but had no idea he'd be so sure of himself, so fervent. "I don't know what to say."

"Are you surprised I'm still in love with you?" Jake crossed the room to sit again and laced his fingers together on the table.

"I didn't expect it. We don't know each other as adults."

"We can get to know each other."

"What do you mean? Like, date?"

He leaned forward. "Rose, I swore to myself for years that if I was lucky enough to have you back, I'd do anything I could to keep you. *Anything*, Rose. If you want me to move, I'll move. You want us to have fifty dogs and a house on a hundred acres and a sanctuary for animals - I'm there. You want to go the opposite way and move to a city somewhere else, tell me when and I'll be packed in an hour.

"The only thing that time away from you has taught me is that I need you. I've been barely above water for the last decade. Then I heard your voice on the phone, and I took the first deep breath in years. And now that you're here, I can breathe again.

"But everything is up to you. I know I'm coming on strong, and I don't want to scare you, I just want to be honest and open. That was my mistake when I was a dumbass teenager who was afraid of his own feelings. My therapist helped me figure out a lot of shit, but mostly that I have to walk through my emotions, not run away."

Rose had avoided his gaze, but that last sentence surprised her enough to look up at him. "You have a therapist?"

"Yeah, I've been going once, sometimes twice a month for the last few years."

"That's incredible."

"Finally took your advice."

Rose choked out a small laugh. "I forgot I'd told you that you need therapy."

"Only once, and it was when I had my head up my ass. You were right."

"Can you say that again into a recording device?"

He rolled his eyes. "Haha. And I know, I do, that I can come on too strong. I want to make sure you know that I love you, I will always love you, always been in love with you. But you need to know that the decision to give us a chance is up to you."

Could she say yes to giving them another chance? She'd never loved anyone else the way she'd loved Jake. She walked out on her own wedding, not just because Henry wasn't the right man, but because she'd needed to find out if Jake felt the same.

Her fear of rejection the last few months had been paralyzing to the point that she hadn't once reached out. But here he was, promising her the moon and stars if she asked for it. Was it enough?

"If I say no? If I don't want more than a few nights of sex and that's it?"

Jake leaned back in his chair. "I don't know if I can have you in my bed for any length of time and let you go, so I can't promise a few nights of just sex. But if you don't want to give us another go, then when your power comes back on, I'll drive you home, make sure you get your car back, and leave you be."

It was Rose's turn to sit back. He hadn't tried to argue or try to convince her to give them another shot. "That's not what I expected you to say."

"Rose, you should know that I'd never force you to be with me. That's creepy and breaks a few laws. If you tell me you don't want to be with me, I'll find a way to deal with it. But I don't think it's what you want."

She met his gaze, those green eyes full of certainty. "You don't?"

"No, do you know why?"

"No." It was the truth. How could he know what she wanted when they didn't know each other anymore?

"Because you let me bring you to my house after you got the message that your power was out. You didn't insist I take you somewhere else."

"I did suggest my parent's house."

"Yes, and when we both agreed that wasn't a good option because of that death-trap of a hill, you didn't fight my idea about coming here."

"No, I didn't," she said quietly.

"So, I'm going to ask the question outright so we're clear on where we stand."

Butterflies erupted in her belly.

"Do you want to see if there's still something between us?"

She swallowed. "What would that look like?"

"We have a few days of being pretty stuck together. Let's have a trial run. Let's catch up, talk, spend our days together and get to know each other again. See if we like who the other turned into."

"And our nights?"

Jake's eyes darkened, and a muscle feathered in his jaw. "If you're willing to give this a try, to see if there's still something here, then I know what I'd want to do, but that's up to you."

Rose couldn't think of a downside to his offer. A trial run relationship would have sounded ridiculous if anyone else had suggested it, but coming from Jake it sounded logical. They were trapped in the house for at least another day, why not take advantage of the chance? If it didn't work out or they discovered they can't stand each other anymore, then better to know now instead of years down the line, right?

If he could offer up his vulnerability, then she could do the same.

And spending the next night or two tangled up with Jake and exploring every inch of his toned body was the cherry on top of the metaphorical sundae that she couldn't help but bite into.

"I would love nothing more than to spend the next few days with you." She smiled at him. Her heart felt lighter as he grinned in return.

"And…I know exactly how I want us to spend our nights." Rose was sure he could hear her heartbeat as she got up and moved to stand in front of him.

Jake started to reach for her hip but paused in midair. "What do you want, Rose?"

She nudged his legs apart with her knee and straddled his lap. His breath hitched and he gripped her hips as he looked up at her, hope in his eyes.

Jake.

Her Jake.

Rose brushed a hand through his hair. He closed his eyes, as if to savor the feeling.

"I want you, Jake. I want to know how we can make this work between us."

"Rose, I—"

She put a finger on his lips, and he immediately obeyed the unspoken command.

"No talking yet. That's for tomorrow, in the daylight. The sun is down, which means it's not time for talking."

He nodded. "And how are we going to spend our nights, Rose?" His voice was thick with desire, gruff and low.

"I've missed you, Jake." Her words were barely above a whisper. She touched her forehead to his.

"I've missed you too, beautiful."

Rose pressed her lips against his. She couldn't stop the whimper that escaped as he threaded one of his hands through her hair to cup the back of her head.

Jake froze and started to pull back. "I'm sorry, I shouldn't have—"

"No, it's amazing. Do it again and more." Rose gripped his shoulders and rocked her hips against him.

"Thank fuck," he whispered as he cupped her head again and pulled her in for a crushing kiss. His other hand gripped her hip, guiding her to rock back and forth on his lap.

She rocked against him, her body on fire with need. It had been so long since she'd felt this kind of passion. Jake had been the one who coaxed her desire to the surface so many years ago. Now it was as though her body recognized him and woke up from a slumber. She'd never had this intense of a reaction to anyone else, only him.

Only Jake.

He broke away from her lips to kiss down her neck. When Jake got to the collar of the shirt she'd borrowed, he moved his hands to tug at the bottom. Rose pulled it over her head and tossed it on the table next to them, her breasts bare.

Jake stared at her, silent. Nervous something was wrong, Rose started to cover up, but Jake reached out a hand first. He brushed the back of his fingers along the outer curve of her breast and lifted his gaze to hers. His lips were parted, and there was clear need in his eyes.

"You're so beautiful."

She grinned and kissed him again, deep and full. He matched her enthusiasm; slipped his hands under her thighs. Jake lifted her ever so slightly, and Rose adjusted so she hovered just over his lap. Jake moved the hem of the borrowed boxers aside and waited. Every muscle in Rose's body was tight and aching, and she throbbed with need. Need for him to fill her, need to chase release.

"Yes," she whispered against his lips, rocking her hips to emphasize her desire.

Jakes' reply was to brush his knuckles against her most sensitive spot. Sparks flitted through her body. She rolled her head back, eyes closed.

Jake's hand disappeared as he kissed her exposed neck, soft and slow - with a flick of his tongue at each spot before he moved on to the next. His slow descent turned her into a writhing mess, bucking her hips looking for any kind of touch or friction.

Jake chuckled. Rose didn't have time to ask what was funny because he slid his knuckles across her clit again and then down the center of her body.

He growled. "Fuck, Rose. You're so wet for me."

Every nerve ending on her body was on fire. "Jake." It was all she could to breathe his name.

"Yes, beautiful?"

The steady pressure he kept on her clit combined with the teasing strokes of his fingers at her slit was an exquisite torment.

"Please." Rose tried to slide herself onto his fingers, but he was too quick. She whined at the lack of him.

"Use your words, Rose. Tell me what you need."

The growl of a command sent shivers up her spine. "You. I need you."

"To do what?" A quick press against her clit as he asked the question. She whimpered. Her entire body was taut, and her control began to fray at the edges.

"I don't know, I just need you." The confession came out in a rush of breath and moans.

"You have me, Rose. All of me - every single piece of me is yours."

She looked at him, at the honesty and desire mixed in his eyes. She kissed him, long and hard. Rose moaned when Jake finally slipped one, then two fingers inside and moved them in a tantalizingly slow circular motion.

"Fuck, beautiful. You're so ready for me." He moved his fingers in unhurried strokes. Rose ground herself against him, her body searching for more. More pressure, more friction, more pleasure, just more.

"That's it, beautiful. Take what you need."

Her breathing uneven, Rose buried her face in his neck, and dug her fingers into his back. Pressure started to build low in her abdomen, and Rose chased the feeling, rotating her hips with Jake's ministrations. The pressure built and built until she thought her body would implode.

"I can feel you fluttering around my fingers, Rose. Do you want me to stop teasing your perfect pussy and make you come for me?"

"Yes. Please, Jake. I'm so close. Please," she breathed.

Jake used his other hand to play with her clit again. Pleasure jolted through her body with every stroke of his fingers.

"Don't stop, Jake, please don't stop."

"Not a chance. I want you to come all over my hand. You're so fucking beautiful when you lose control, Rose." He growled in her ear, "That's it, yes."

She cried out his name as her orgasm tore through her, pleasure radiating to every part of her. Jake whispered words of praise in her ear. "That's it, yes, right there. Keep coming for me, yes, just like that." He continued to tease out her pleasure with his expert fingers until her legs shook and she collapsed against him.

He kissed the side of her head. "Good girl."

All but limp, Rose warmed at the praise. She turned to kiss him and caught the expression of awe on his face.

Rose could barely let out a chuckle. "That was amazing," she said on an exhale, and sat up to rest her legs on his lap.

"You are amazing."

Rose put her fingers under his chin to tilt his face up to hers and kissed him, long and slow. A kiss meant to convey her appreciation and give her body space to recover. The feel of his hands gripping her hips had the opposite effect. She wanted him again. She wanted to sink down on him and ride him until he called out her name and they were both spent.

Rose broke the kiss and stood. She slid the borrowed boxers off and stepped out of them. There was a feral grin on Jake's face as he watched her every move. Her body again burned with need, and she ached to have him fill her.

"Take off your pants."

CHAPTER 6

Rose kept her eyes on the swipe of Jake's tongue as he licked his bottom lip. He raked his gaze down and back up her body. She shivered, and not from the chill in the air.

After what felt like ages, Jake stood, and pulled his shirt over his head. His broad shoulders were complemented by a muscular chest, which was sprinkled with dark hair. Jake had grown into himself, indeed.

She didn't try to hide her desire as she trailed her eyes down to his abs – toned in a way that happens with manual labor instead of time in a gym. And lickable. So very lickable. There was a trail that disappeared under his pants, and Rose wanted to follow it.

Jake unbuckled his belt and pulled it free from his jeans in one smooth movement. Rose's mouth went dry as he undid the button and zipper and got rid of them. His boxer briefs disappeared next.

Before Rose could reach for him, Jake was on his knees in front of her, gliding his fingers up her calves as he placed reverent kisses along her hips and lower belly. She buried her fingers in his hair, his name a breath on her lips. "Oh, Jake."

He reached the back of her thighs with his hands and nudged them open. Rose obeyed the soft command, her body ready for whatever he wanted.

Jake kissed his way down one hip, along the top of her thigh until he came to the apex between her thighs - where she was wet and needy.

He exhaled a soft breath over her. Rose moaned at the sensation, and then cried out in frustration when he pressed his lips to her opposite inner thigh.

Jake laughed. "Someone's in a hurry."

She tugged on his hair, enough to make him pull his head back and look up at her. The sight of him on his knees before her, his full lips slightly parted, eyes full of desire, was almost too much to bear.

"I. Need. Your. Cock."

"As you wish," he chuckled. Rose grinned as he remembered her favorite movie. She released the grip on his hair as he stood. She put a hand on his chest.

"Sit."

"We need a condom first."

"Right." Rose didn't know how she'd forgotten about it.

"I have some." Jake gripped her chin, his hold gentle but commanding. Her pussy throbbed. He brought his mouth to her ear and growled, "Don't fucking move." He kissed her mouth hard as if to emphasize his point.

"Mhm," she was breathless again as he disappeared behind her. The chill in the air brought goosebumps to her body, her nipples already peaked and aching.

He tapped her ass when he came back, condom already on.

"Sit," she repeated, her command weaker than earlier.

Still, he obeyed with that grin on his face, and splayed his legs open enough for her to sit comfortably. Jake palmed his cock and pumped it a few times. Rose watched the movement of his fist up and down, up and down. She was so transfixed on the movements, it became difficult to breathe, until Jake growled.

"Bring your sweet pussy over here and get on my cock, beautiful."

Rose grinned and straddled him again, her hands on his shoulders. She hovered above his lap, lining herself up with his cock.

Jake cupped the back of her head and brought his mouth to hers. This kiss was gentle, but Rose wanted harder. She dug her nails into his shoulders and lowered herself onto his cock.

Jake met her gaze and Rose saw his desire for her in the green depths. "Fuuuck." He drew out the word as she sank down. "Ah, that's it, slow and steady." He was thick enough that she had to roll her hips a couple of times to fully seat herself on him.

"Fuck. Yes." Jake didn't break her gaze, just gripped her hips tighter.

The feel of him inside her again after so much time apart was exquisite. She wanted more. Needed more. Needed to move with him buried deep. Driven entirely by her body, Rose leaned back and rocked her hips.

Jake watched her every move beneath hooded eyes, one hand behind her to keep her steady. He trailed the other along her body as she moved on him; her skin ignited wherever he touched - along the curve of her breast, her belly, back up to her breasts. He pinched her nipple and then leaned in and took the sore peak into his mouth, soothing with his tongue.

Rose couldn't find words. She rocked her hips again, and again, and the tip of his cock brushed that perfect spot again, and again.

Jake looked down between their bodies and groaned. "Look at you. Fuck, Rose, you take me so well. Look at your pussy wrapped around my cock."

Rose whimpered. Pressure and pleasure built and built, coiled tight. "Jake. Please. I'm so close."

"I know, beautiful. I know." Jake put his thumb to her mouth, and she opened to suck on it. He groaned, "Fuck."

She released it with a pop. Jake kissed her, devoured her, and pressed his thumb to her clit.

Rose's entire universe narrowed to her body, the way Jake's cock brushed against the magical spot, and the press of his thumb. He expertly teased and played with the small bundle of nerves until Rose was nothing more than wordless sounds and frantic movements.

The pressure in her body started to release, a flutter low her belly and she clenched around his cock.

"That's it, yes." But he kept teasing and toying with her, that orgasm just out of reach.

"Jake," she pleaded. "Please." Her hips bucked and he relented. Whatever hold he'd had on his own desire snapped. He matched her hip rolls with thrusts and drove himself harder and deeper against that spot again and again, and his fingers rolled against her clit in a circle.

Rose thought she would die from it. Her orgasm exploded through her, this one faster and more intense than the first.

Jake wrapped his arms around her and held her close, the side of his face buried between her breasts. His became were erratic, and he pumped again and again, until he cried out and his body shuddered beneath hers, his cock twitching inside of her.

He relaxed his grip and stroked her hair. He kissed her temple, her cheek, and then her lips. "That was incredible."

Rose murmured her agreement.

"We should clean up. Maybe...watch a movie?" He hadn't stopped stroking her hair, and Rose had never felt such comfort and peace, especially after such an intense experience.

"Mm," was the only response she could muster.

He chuckled as he lifted her off his lap. Her legs not quite recovered, Rose gripped the table for support. When her muscles stopped quivering, she dressed.

"You know, the shower in the en suite has a really great showerhead and excellent water pressure." Jake had pulled his boxer briefs up, his jeans still in his hands. Rose had barely managed to get the boxers on.

"Oh really?" She made a show of thinking about it. "Is it big enough for two?" She took a few shaky steps in the direction of his bedroom.

"In fact, it is. I remodeled recently and made it much bigger."

Rose grinned and backed up another few steps. "I think I can be persuaded to use your shower to clean up, if the right offer came along."

Jake caught up to her, and Rose squealed as he wrapped his arms around her waist and lifted her into a fireman's carry. "Oh, I'm not just offering, beautiful. I'm insisting." He smacked her ass.

The sting was a delightful small pain. One she knew promised pleasure soon.

Rose sighed dramatically in an attempt to hide her giggle. "If you insist, who am I to argue?"

CHAPTER 7

Another two orgasms and a shower later, Rose snuggled against Jake in his king-sized bed under a comforter and could not imagine a better place to be during a blizzard - or any night, really. A movie they'd already seen together forever ago played on the mounted screen across the room.

They'd explored each other's bodies until the hot water started to run out. Then Jake had instructed Rose to get comfortable in bed while he fed and walked Daisy one more time.

Daisy had followed Jake down the hall when they came inside and had curled up on the foot of the bed.

"I'm pretty sure this was one of our first date movies," Jake said as he stroked her hair.

Rose adjusted a pillow between her head and Jake's body. "Mm, I think it was one we watched after we'd been dating a while."

"Maybe." Jake was quiet for a moment. "My favorite movie is whatever was playing when I hid whipped cream in the couch and you let me lick it off your body."

Oh, Rose remembered. "That was a fun night." It had been full of teasing and giggles and exploration in pursuit of pleasure.

Jake moved his hand from her hair to her shoulder and stroked down her arm. Rose fought against a delightful shiver.

"Mm. I'm glad you remember it too. It's one of my favorite memories."

"Mine, too." Rose reached across his chest for his free hand. She entwined their fingers together and squeezed.

"I didn't mean to break the No Talking at Night rule."

"I'll let it slide just this once," she said.

"That sounds suspiciously like an invitation to break the rule again." Jake brushed his fingers against her breast and Rose leaned into it.

"I forgot how much of a rule breaker you can be." She tilted her head to look up at him. His eyes had darkened with desire, and her body flushed under the intensity of his gaze.

"We can take a break if you need to, beautiful."

"What makes you think I need a break yet?"

"I'm hoping you don't but wanted to make sure you knew you could press the figurative stop button."

Rose sat up all the way and climbed on top of him, her knees on either side of his hips. She leaned down to kiss him, his mouth soft and welcoming.

"I haven't reached my limit yet, Jake. And I don't know that I ever will when it comes to us."

"Thank fuck," he growled. Jake wrapped his arms around her, held her tight, and rolled her onto her back.

Rose loved the feel of his strong body on hers, the weight of him pressing down. She sighed as he kissed his way down her neck, until he once again came to the collar of a borrowed shirt.

He made a sound of annoyance and tugged at the hem. Rose let him pull it over her head. "We need to get you into one of my dress shirts."

"Why is that?"

"Buttons."

She laughed and stretched her arms above her head, eyes

closed, and reveled in the sensations of Jake's lips and tongue along her body. He disappeared for long enough that Rose opened her eyes and sat up to search for him.

Jake had scooped up Daisy and moved her to the cushions and chair across the room. The look on Daisy's face was pure 'why did you move me,' incredulity. "You're a good girl, but we need the bed to ourselves, pretty girl."

"Now that's sweet," Rose said as Jake gave Daisy a kiss on the head and scratched behind her ears.

"She wasn't in a great location." Jake prowled back to the bed and nibbled his way up her legs.

Rose let her head fall back on the pillows, and wondered if they would ever get anything else done if it felt this incredible to explore each other.

Jake had grown into his height, maturing from tall and gangly to tall with broad shoulders, strong biceps, and a muscular chest. Rose had plans of her own to kiss and lick her way across his body. But for now, she enjoyed Jake's expert exploration of her own curves and muscles.

Rose moaned his name as he licked her thigh and then nibbled her hip. He replied by sucking on the inner thigh of the opposite leg. Jake slipped a finger along the slick wetness of her opening. Rose moaned again as Jake continued to tease and kiss and lick everywhere but where her body ached for his mouth.

Their earlier activities had her body primed and ready, and it only took a few seconds. after Jake wrapped his lips around her clit and flicked it with his tongue once, twice, three times, and her body splintered into bursts of pleasure.

Jake hummed in approval and then slid two fingers into her already convulsing pussy. "That's it beautiful, keep coming for me." He stroked and worked her through the exquisite pleasure, so incredible a few tears rolled down her face.

Jake eased his ministrations. "You still with me, beautiful?"

"Mm, ngh uh," was all Rose could manage.

He chuckled. "Here, have some water." Jake passed her the water bottle from his nightstand. Grateful, Rose sat up and took a few mouthfuls, the cold smacking her senses back into place.

"Thank you," she managed.

"For the water or the orgasms?" Jake kissed her forehead before he took a drink of water and returned it to the table.

"Both, Mr. Snark."

He laughed as he settled next to her and propped himself up on his arm. "Would you like a break yet?"

"Are you trying to wear me out via multiple orgasms? Is that a goal here? Because I think I can get on board with that."

"It seems a fun way to pass the night, doesn't it?"

Rose hummed and leaned up to kiss him. "Indeed, but I think there should be an equitable distribution of orgasms. Don't you? And I do believe it's your turn." She pushed herself up and maneuvered them until Jake was on his back and she settled on top of his hips.

Jake's exhale when she nibbled her way down his jaw and neck made her feel powerful and sexy. Rose reached between them to touch and tease his cock with her fingers. His hips bucked, and she smiled to herself.

His chest was muscular and defined, and she loved the tickle of the patch of hair smattered across his muscles. She made her way down his stomach and abdomen. There was a lovely softness above the hardness of his abs, and she took great care to nibble and suck and kiss everywhere she could.

Jake wove his fingers into her hair and held on. "Is that okay?" He asked, his grip loosened a bit.

"Mhm," was her only reply and she continued her way down his body.

Rose took her time before she finally got to his hard length. She took the tip of him into her mouth and Jake's body bucked.

"Fuck." The word came out as a gasp. "You look so fucking

perfect with your mouth around my cock. Fuck." Jake exhaled the last word.

Rose hummed at the praise, grinned, and flicked her tongue out across his tip, and tasted a salty sweetness. Emboldened by his body's reaction to her ministrations, Rose wrapped one of her hands around the base of him and pumped in small strokes, squeezing ever so slightly on the descent.

"If you don't stop, Rose …"

She hardly paused as she looked up at him, as if to ask if he really wanted her to stop.

"I'm not going to last much longer, fuck." His head fell back on the pillow. "Rose, I'm going to fucking come in your mouth if you don't stop."

Rose didn't stop.

She pumped his cock with one hand, licked and swirled her tongue around his tip, and held herself up with her other hand on his thigh. She gently dug her nails into his leg, and Jake gripped her hair tighter.

"Rose, fuck, I'm going—" Jake's words turned into a moan as his hips jerked up and his orgasm hit. Rose sucked and licked and swallowed everything he gave her.

She only stopped when he gasped and said, "Please, too much."

Rose grinned up at him, his green eyes half closed from pleasure.

It was definitely a fun way to pass the night.

CHAPTER 8

Sunlight glittered across the top of the snow in Jake's front yard. There were several feet of it, and drifts had blown over night. Jake's truck was covered, and the snow on the ground reached above the bumpers.

Rose stared out the window at the serene morning, grateful for the mug of hot coffee in her hands. "I haven't seen snow like this in years."

"Me neither." Jake came up behind her, wrapped his arms around her waist and kissed her temple. "It's going to be a pain in the ass to clean up, though."

"I'll help," she offered.

"You'll do no such thing." Rose nudged him but he continued, "Hell, I only went out long enough to clear a path and space for Daisy to go out and do her business."

"When did you do that?"

"While you were sleeping in."

Guilt over sleeping when he was out in the cold and snow crept in. "Oh. I would have helped."

"I wouldn't have let you. You needed the sleep after last night's…exercises."

She blushed and looked over and spotted the black dog on Jake's large L-shaped couch. Daisy wasn't curled up in a tight ball like the day before. She was on her belly, legs out in comfortable angles, her head on a pillow. Her brown eyes watched them from across the space. "She looks comfortable."

"She settled right in, didn't she?"

Rose leaned back against Jake and admitted, "She's not the only one."

"Yeah?" Jake turned Rose to face him. She smiled up at him as he brushed a hair out of her face. "You're feeling settled in?"

"Maybe it's crazy to say, but," she shrugged. "Yeah. It feels like we've picked up where we left off, but without the teenage angst and drama."

"I think so, too."

"Though, you're a lot more secure and stable than I am these days."

Confusion etched his face. "What do you mean?"

Rose hesitated. She took a step back and leaned against the counter behind her. Jake let her step out of his arms but didn't move otherwise.

She took a deep breath before admitting, "My life has been a mess for months. For the first time since I realized I couldn't marry Henry, I feel — secure. Safe."

"I'm glad to hear that."

"You are? You don't care that if we decide this —" she motioned between them — "has staying power, I come with a lot of baggage, both literal and figurative?"

Jake shook his head. "Everyone has baggage, Rose. I'll help you carry yours if you'll help me with mine."

"Of course, I'd help with yours. I just…" she trailed off as the realization of how much additional emotional labor she'd had to do in previous relationships struck her. Even with Henry.

"What, beautiful? You just…what?"

"I, I don't know. Nobody else has ever been so willing to be an equal partner on the heavier emotional stuff that comes up."

"Rose, I've known and loved you since we were teenagers, and then loved you from afar while you were with another man. Why the hell wouldn't I be supportive and give you whatever you need from me now that you're here?"

No other relationship, from first dates that never got to a second all the way to her almost marriage, had ever been equitable in the emotional work. There was always, always, a layer of 'you help me with my shit, but I can't help you the same way' caveat. Not even Henry. While he'd been supportive of her and always had a shoulder for her to cry on, he'd never stood up to his overly-opinionated and emotionally manipulative mother until after Rose had left him at the altar.

And here was Jake, her first love, offering equal support, love, and holding space for her.

"Thank you," she choked out, before tears welled and rolled down her cheeks. Rose let Jake wrap his arms around her and pull her against his chest. She buried her face into his soft shirt, the muscles hard beneath the flannel. Rose let herself cry and sank into the quiet strength Jake provided.

He stroked her hair and back as she sobbed, the motion comforting. She cried even harder. Jake never wavered.

Once the tears slowed and stopped, her breath still hitching, Rose stepped back. Before she could wipe her tears away, Jake cupped her face in his hands and made her look up at him. He gently brushed his thumbs across her cheeks and kissed her forehead.

Rose had never felt more cherished.

"I'm sorry I got your shirt all wet," she sniffled.

"Not something you need to apologize for, ever."

Tears threatened to fall again, and she cleared her throat in an attempt to stave them off. "I'm going to go wash my face. I'll be right back."

Jake stepped out of the way for her to pass. "I'll make us something to eat. Egg sandwiches?"

"Perfect." Rose disappeared before she cried again. Jake remembered one of her favorite comfort foods. The man was too good to be true.

She stepped into the bathroom, closed the door, and leaned against it. Rose wanted to be brave enough to see if they could make an actual relationship work between them as adults, to make sure they had lasting power now. To be brave enough to find out if whatever was between them wasn't just physical attraction combined with nostalgic emotion.

She took a few minutes to breathe before she splashed cold water on her face and dried off. The scent of egg sandwiches and bacon beckoned her back to the kitchen.

"That smells delicious," she remarked.

"Sit, sit. I'll bring everything over in a second." Jake busied himself plating the sandwiches and bacon. There was already a bowl of bananas on the small table in the breakfast nook.

Rose kissed his cheek as she passed him and took a seat. She flushed at the memory of what they'd done the night before, at that very table.

She looked out the window for a distraction, and spotted a female cardinal huddled in a nest in the branches of the snow-covered bush. Her mate wasn't far, over in the next bush. She and her late grandmother shared a love for cardinals, and Rose had spent many weekends doing puzzles of the birds with her. In the years since her grandmother had passed, Rose believed spotting a cardinal was a visit or a sign from her favorite person.

Jake brought the food over and sat across from her at the table.

The over easy eggs on an everything bagel was perfect. She smiled up at him. "Thanks."

Jake waved his hand and took a bite of his egg and plain bagel. "It's nothing," he said between bites.

Rose shook her head. "No, it's not 'nothing.' You making me something to eat is very much something. I appreciate it." She took a bite and the combination of toasted bagel crunch with the softness of the eggs was perfect. "It's delicious."

"You're acting as if nobody's ever cooked for you before." Jake's expression went from joking to incredulous as his own words hung for a moment. "Wait. Are you telling me that no other man has ever made you a meal?"

Rose couldn't look him in the eye. "There were a lot of dinners out or ordered in - delicious food from expensive restaurants. But I was the only one who ever used the kitchen to make something." For a long time, Rose had thought the expensive restaurants and gifts were a direct correlation of the amount of affection held by her partner. Maybe it was true for some, but the gesture of making soup for someone when they're ill, or a comfort breakfast food after a mini breakdown in the kitchen, was much more meaningful and important to Rose.

Jake was quiet for a few heartbeats before he said, "I may not be able to compete financially with other guys out there, but I know how to use my kitchen. What do you want for dinner tonight? I have a freezer in the garage packed with different meats, vegetables in the fridge, and just about any kind of dry goods in the pantry."

"You don't have to—"

"Rose." Jake reached across the table to grasp her hand. "I love to cook, and I love to cook for others. I'm not a trained chef or anything but my food hasn't made anyone sick yet. You deserve for someone to make you a meal."

"You made me breakfast." She didn't know why she kept rejecting his offer, except that it felt unbalanced between them. There wasn't much she could offer in return, at least not while they were trapped in his house by snow.

"An egg sandwich on a toasted bagel, bacon, and some fruit is not what I'm talking about, and I think you know that."

Rose knew Jake stared at her even as she kept her eyes averted and could almost hear the gears turning in his brain. She took another bite of her sandwich and tried to change the subject. Anything to keep him from seeing her thoughts.

"When did you learn how to cook? If memory serves, the most complex thing you used to make was grilled cheese." She thought about the one he'd made last night and added, "A damned good grilled cheese, though."

"When I started living on my own. I didn't want to spend my paycheck on fast food, though there's been plenty of that, too. It was something new to learn and pass the time. Plus, I'd get to eat what I made. And it's a useful skill, and I like to collect those."

"What other useful skills have you collected?" She meant the question in complete innocence, but Jake's expression turned sinful.

"Pretty sure I've demonstrated a few of those skills already." There was a promise of more in his eyes.

Her toes curled, and she wanted to match his playful energy. "Anything outside the bedroom, or have you spent so much time dedicating yourself to the pleasure of female companions that you haven't had time?"

Rose immediately regretted her words and the unintentional meanness in her tone. She'd gotten too comfortable and forgot to keep a lid on her snark. She didn't know how she could have forgotten it was only tolerated by a select few and that she had to tone it down with everyone else. She could smack herself for it.

Jake finished his egg bagel and took a bite of bacon. He locked his gaze on her and said quietly, "I haven't been with anyone in over a year. And I've only been with three women in my life, including you."

"Jake, I'm sorry. I was a bitch. You did nothing to deserve it." In her rush to make amends, it took a few extra seconds for his words to sink in. "Oh, ohh." Shame flooded her, and her cheeks heated. "I should have never said anything — it was supposed to be playful but obviously came out very wrong. I'm sorry I upset you."

Rose barely met his gaze as she spoke but forced herself to hold it. Jake was the last person she wanted to hurt.

"I'd understand if you want me to find a way home or another place to stay." She finally looked down at her plate, waiting for him to banish her or for him to go hide in an office or garage until he calmed down and she apologized again, like the boyfriend she'd had before Henry.

"Why would I want that?"

"Because of what I said."

"But why would I want you to leave? I'm not hurt or offended. Sometimes things come out wrong. We're all human."

Rose nodded slowly, once, not quite believing him.

"Rose, I just got you back in my life. I'm not worried about a sharp tongue, accidental or not. In fact," he stood and moved around the table to kneel next to her chair. "Look at me, please, beautiful."

She twisted herself so she faced him, and he adjusted so he was between her legs. "There isn't a part of you that I won't love. There is no part of yourself that you need to hide from me. I like your sarcasm and biting wit. It keeps me on my toes, and I love never knowing what you're going to say next. Other men might sulk and pout when confronted with a strong, intelligent, beautiful woman way out of their league, but I am not weak. I am enraptured."

"But you were so serious, and you looked like I upset you. That's the last thing I ever want to do," she whispered.

Jake held her thighs and stroked with his thumbs. Not to tease, but to calm and reassure. Rose noticed some of the anxiety dissipate under his touch.

"Then that's on me. I wasn't - am not, upset. I was being honest and wanted you to see my sincerity."

"Oh." Relief inched in and she took a shaky breath. "Do you mind if I ask a question?"

"Definitely. No follow up questions allowed." He winked, and the rest of the worry and tension in her body melted away. "What's your question?"

"Have you really only been with two other women?"

"Yes. You were my first."

She smiled and cupped his cheek. "I knew that. You were mine, too." They'd been each other's first for so many things, both sexual and not. That bond ran deep between them. Rose wanted to find a way to build it up strong enough to weather any storm that may come for them in the future.

He grinned up at her, his eyes alight with mischief. "Backseat of my truck after a movie."

"At the lake," she added. Rose brushed her fingers through his hair. "One of my favorite nights, though I'm not sure I could contort that way again," she laughed.

Jake growled. "That sounds like a challenge. When it's not freezing outside."

"Maybe it is, maybe it isn't."

"Hmm," was his only response.

"Not to ruin the lovely walk down memory lane, but I have another question."

"Sure, but can we move to the couch because this floor is hard on the knees."

CHAPTER 9

They made quick work of the empty plates and settled on the couch.

Daisy had gone in search of water and then curled up on the couch again. She was close but not close enough to pet. Rose cooed at her but didn't make any moves to pet her; she knew how important personal space was, even for dogs.

Rose claimed one end, a pillow propped behind her for comfort against the arm, her legs pulled up in front of her. Jake sat next to her and pulled her legs onto his lap.

"What's your question?" He started to massage her calves, and for a moment or two, Rose forgot about anything else.

"Your hands are magic."

"Another useful skill, you'll notice." Jake winked.

"Mm, definitely. It's competing for top spot in my rankings." Rose stifled a moan as he worked her sore muscles.

"What's it in competition with?" His wicked grin returned. "It's the tongue thing, isn't it? It is, it's the tongue thing."

Rose pushed against his shoulder as he puffed out his chest. "You're pretty cocky right now."

He licked his lips, and then bit his bottom lip. "You have no idea, beautiful." Jake pressed her leg against his lap; his cock was hard through his sweatpants. Rose's mouth went dry, and she pressed her thighs together.

"But daytime is for talking, right?" Jake moved her leg back to where it had been on his thighs.

"Right, right." The wetness between her legs disagreed.

"Your question?" Jake prompted when she was still quiet.

"Oh, yeah. Not to be a wet blanket, but — why only two other women? Most guys I've met have a higher body count. Not that there is anything to be ashamed of — it just surprised me, is all. You're so…talented," she choked on the last word. "I assumed there would have been more partners in order to get to that level of … anyway I'm going to shut up now."

"Thanks for the 'talented' compliment. But that has more to do with the woman who inspires me to find new ways to bring her pleasure than anything else."

Rose rolled her eyes but a secret thrill ran through her.

"I never had much interest in sleeping around, or in casual sex with a bunch of partners."

"Okay. What was special about the two? Were they long relationships?"

"Not really." Jake looked at her and then away, and Rose swore she saw a hint of pain in his eyes. "The first one was a few months after you left for school. All of my friends were telling me I had to get back out there and move on. And after the heartache and depression, I figured it couldn't hurt. I met someone in one of my classes, we exchanged numbers, and went on a few dates before we slept together."

Rose knew she had no right to the jealousy and possessiveness roaring in her head, but it was hard to control, nonetheless. She waited for him to continue, giving him the space he'd given her not that long ago.

"It was — not great. Not bad exactly, but awkward and clumsy and just — not great. We did go out a few more times and tried again, but she stopped returning my texts not long after."

"Rude," Rose's mouth made the decision to speak before her brain had any input.

"Nah, I don't blame her. We weren't a good fit."

"Hm," was all she said. If it was this difficult for Rose to listen to stories about a couple of dates and bad sex, she couldn't imagine how Jake must have felt when she broke down about the failures in her relationship with Henry.

He looked down and continued, his voice softer. "The second one was the only time I had a one-night stand. Not my finest hour."

"You don't have to tell me about it if you don't want to, Jake."

"It's not that. I don't mind sharing with you, and in fact it feels good to connect. That's what we want this weekend or however many days we have to be, right? Honesty about who we are now, how we got here, and seeing if we can find a way forward together?"

Rose nodded. "But I don't want you to feel obligated to share something painful that you're not ready to talk about yet. That's me being honest about who I am now, Jake."

"Sharing my life over the last few years with you is not an obligation, Rose. It's a privilege I take seriously."

There were no words to describe how she felt. Rose pulled him down to her and pressed her lips to his. A quick kiss to express all of the emotion she couldn't voice. "You are an amazing man, Jake, and I am lucky to know you, let alone spend any part of my life with you."

Jake cupped his hand at the nape of her neck and pressed his lips to hers. It wasn't frenzied or rushed, but deliberate and deep.

"I'm the luckiest motherfucker on the planet. I still can't believe you're here," he whispered against her mouth. He kissed her forehead and sat up again. "Especially because I never thought I'd get a second chance with you." He pulled her legs onto his lap again, but simply held them there.

"What do you mean?"

"I fucked up so badly all those years ago. I should never have walked away during that stupid fight. I knew it then, too. But I was so wrapped up in my own crap and fear of not being good enough for you combined with the insecurity of you going away to college and possibly meeting someone else…" He trailed off. "I couldn't see that I needed to fight harder to keep you, keep us."

"Oh, Jake. We were both young, stupid, and didn't know any better."

"I know. But then you left for school, and I heard that you were dating other people. I figured maybe I hadn't meant the same to you as you had to me, but I could *not* get rid of the ache in my chest no matter how hard I tried. Then you were with Henry. The night I found out you were engaged was one of the worst nights of my life."

"Jake, I'm sor—"

"No, don't apologize," he cut her off. "You have no reason and nothing to be sorry for. Not a single damn thing. Okay?"

She nodded and motioned for him to continue.

"I'd always known you were out of my league, and it looked like Henry was someone worthy of you. At least from the outside. With that ring on your finger, I believed you were out of my reach forever. I spent that night just sitting and staring at the wall."

Her heart broke at the image. She reached for his hand and squeezed it.

"A week or so later, some of the guys from work dragged me to the bar and kept buying me drinks. It was their way of cheering me up. It didn't work. Instead, I got shitfaced, hooked up with a girl in the bathroom, and went home with her."

Jealousy flared bright and hot in Rose's chest. She forced it down as he continued.

"She was kind, I think, but I never called her after that night. I didn't want a reminder of my lowest moment, or of what led me there. I'd planned to be out of town for the weekend of your wedding, but plans fell through. That's when we saw each other at the store."

Rose remembered. It had been the catalyst to make her rethink everything she was about to do.

"I wished you well, and I meant it, but my heart was in pieces at the thought of you spending your life with another man." Jake finally met her gaze. "But then you didn't marry him."

"No, I didn't," she whispered.

"And you're here, in my house and my arms, and in my bed."

"Yes."

"It feels like a dream, and I hope I don't wake up."

Rose smiled. "It does. Being here with you" - she looked around the living room, clearly designed with comfort as the top priority - "it feels like coming home. For the first time in I don't even know how long, I feel safe. I feel like I'm on solid ground, even if sometimes I'm scared it will fall out from underneath me if I say the wrong thing, or forget to pretend I had a good day, or can't pretend I'm okay if I'm not."

"You never have to hide any part of yourself from me. I'm sorry you felt you had to do that in the past with…others."

Rose sorted through her thoughts before she spoke again, examining and deciding what to say.

"It wasn't just romantic relationships, though. I've been making myself smaller in order not to be considered 'too much,' 'too opinionated,' 'too loud,' or taking up too much space, for years."

"Why?" Jake's voice was soft, not accusatory, or incredulous.

"I've been told over and over, in so many different ways, that I'm too 'insert adjective here.' Eventually it took a toll, and I learned I could only be my full self around certain people.

Everyone else only got pieces of me, carefully curated to match their expectations."

"I'm furious you were treated that way. You should never feel like you need to squeeze into a box made by someone else or create some alternate version in order to be more palatable for other people." The sincerity in his voice was clear.

"I've been working on that. It's hard to unlearn bad habits, so to speak."

"Good. I'll kick anyone's ass that tells you some bullshit like that."

Rose laughed. "You'd have been helpful against my first boss. But you don't need to do that." Jake opened his mouth to say something else, but Rose held up a hand. "My point is that I have never needed to do that with you. I've always been safe to be myself. I forgot what that was like, until you rescued me and Daisy over there from the blizzard."

"Good. You are safe, and I never want you to be anyone except yourself." He kissed her forehead.

"The conversation we had at the store changed the way I looked at what I was about to do, who I was about to marry and spend my life with. It was the catalyst for everything."

Jake didn't reply; he just trailed his hands along her calves, quiet again.

"What are you thinking about so intently?"

"Hm? Oh," he laughed. "Uh, honestly, I was wondering how soon we can move your things into the house." Jake glanced at her, his expression wary.

"You want me to move in? It hasn't even been two days."

"If I didn't think it'd scare you away, I'd ask you to marry me."

"Jake." Rose didn't know how to process what he said. "You're that sure? Even though we've barely spent time together as adults?"

"Absolutely. You're still the same person I fell in love with in high school, just more grown into yourself. Like an upgrade to the system, you know? The core of who you are and what makes you great — your kindness, intelligence, wit, humor — is still there, but with the extra bonus of confidence in yourself. Plus, you look damn good in my clothes and even better naked in my bed."

She rolled her eyes. "You're ridiculous, you know that?"

"Maybe, but it's all true. Tell me you don't feel the same — that no matter what happens, we'll be able to get through it if we're together."

She couldn't deny that she wanted to be with Jake, but there were other things to consider. Things they hadn't talked about yet.

"Isn't it too soon? We haven't technically started dating."

"I'd rather be too soon than too late. I don't want to fuck this up again. I'm not going anywhere unless you tell me to."

"I'm scared," she confessed.

"Me, too." Jake continued to massage her legs as he paused.

Rose didn't know how to fill the silence, so she didn't. But then Jake spoke again, and she couldn't have loved him more if she tried.

"What are you scared of? Maybe if we talk about our fears, we can come up with a plan together."

"You go first." She didn't know how to tell him that she was scared of him giving up on their relationship like he did before. It was hard to let go of the fear of him leaving if there was any kind of obstacle to their relationship. Or that she was scared of how unbalanced things were between them.

Jake took a deep breath before he answered. "I'm scared I'm not good enough for you. That you'll wake up one day and see what I offer - a simple life without many expensive gifts and fancy cars, and you'll decide it's not enough."

Rose pulled her legs off of Jake's lap and crossed them in front of her before she reached for his hands. "I had that life already. I had the fancier car and the nice apartment and expensive meals and gifts. I was fucking miserable. I woke up and decided I didn't want *that* life. What you offer is more important. You have more emotional intelligence than most people I know, and you have made me feel more cherished, heard, validated, and loved in the short time I've been here than any of my ex's ever have."

"You deserve everything, Rose. Even the stuff I can't provide." He looked away for a moment and wiped at his face.

"I don't want a big, fancy, empty-of-emotional-connection life. I want you." She kissed his hand and smiled at him. "I will remind you of that any time you need, okay?"

"Deal," he replied. "Your turn."

She swallowed. If Jake could be open and honest, then she could, too. "I'm afraid that you'll walk away again. I know you've told me over and over that you won't, but fear is irrational. And I'm afraid of losing myself in another relationship."

"I'm going to address the second part of that first, okay?"

Rose nodded.

Jake leaned forward and pressed his forehead to hers. "I will not let you get lost. I see you and I love you, and don't want you to become some automaton trophy. I'll push you, challenge you, and hold you when you need me to. But I won't let you get lost."

Tears sprang in her eyes, and she fought to keep them from falling. She nodded, not able to form words. Jake pressed a kiss to her cheek before he sat up.

"Is there anything I can do or promise to make you less worried about me leaving?"

She'd known even last night that she wanted to trust him again, enough to spend a lifetime together, and had spent hours last night contemplating that exact question. It had kept her from sleep, which was why she'd slept in so late that morning.

Her solution had been a question of her own. "What do you imagine our life will look like?" Rose knew that if his vision of their life together aligned with hers, she had no room to doubt him.

"Well, a lot like the last day. But with some reality and disagreements and fights and working through it together. Like we're doing right now." He squeezed her hands. "What do you imagine?"

She beamed. "More of this, too. Everything you said. This house. More dogs, because we're keeping Daisy, and a small wedding."

Daisy looked up at her name, tail wagging. "Sound good to you, pretty girl?" Rose laughed when she yawned and went back to sleep.

He grinned back at her. "Easy, done. You stay, Daisy stays. Anything else?"

"Where do you fall on the subject of kids?" She was hesitant to share her own uncertainty about having kids. It had been a major pain point in her almost-marriage, mostly because of pressure from her overbearing almost-mother-in-law.

"I don't really know, to be honest. I hadn't thought about kids because I didn't think I'd ever get married."

"You didn't?"

"If you weren't going to be my life partner, why bother? Nobody else measured up."

"Jake."

He shrugged. "Just being honest. And that's irrelevant now because you're here. Tell me how you feel about kids. Do you want to have them?"

"I'm not sure, either. I think I'd rather start out having a bunch of dogs and revisit the topic later."

"Solid plan."

Relief flooded her body. "You'd be happy if it was just us and dogs?"

"I'd be happy if it was just you, me, and a cardboard box."

She laughed again. "Okay, weirdo. But I need us to have dogs."

"As many as we can responsibly care for. Plus, we can foster more."

There was one dream Rose had kept to herself for a very long time, since she was a kid. An animal sanctuary. A large piece of land with different fenced areas for different animals, but especially dogs – the ones nobody would take a chance on, the ones people had given up on, the ones that went overlooked in the shelters.

Rose had voiced the idea once to her mom, who had almost always been supportive of whatever Rose wanted. But her mother had been so dismissive of the idea that Rose had never been confident enough to mention it to anyone else.

Until now. If she was going to spend her life with Jake, then she needed to know where he stood on such a large project. It would impact every other part of their life.

"How do you feel about creating a sanctuary for animals?"

"I'm in." He didn't hesitate.

"That was fast."

"I've been working with the local rescues for a few years, and I'd love to create my own. *Our* own," he amended. "I think it'd be a great labor of love for us to tackle and build together."

That was everything Rose needed to know. They could work out anything else that came their way, together.

"Then, yes."

"Yes?" Hope flared bright in his green eyes.

"I'll move in, and I'll marry you."

Jake whooped and almost tackled her in his enthusiasm to kiss her. She laughed and wrapped an arm around his neck and the other on his face as he pressed her back into the couch cushion.

Then he pushed himself up. "Hang on. I'll be right back." Jake jumped over the back of the couch and disappeared.

"What just happened? Where are you going?!" She called after him.

"Don't move!" His shout echoed from the back of the house.

Jake all but ran into the living room, sat on the couch, and scooped her onto his lap.

Rose let him maneuver and settle her on his thighs and, once she was comfortable, asked, "What is happening right now?"

"This," he said, and held up a small velvet box.

"How…how?" Rose couldn't get words out as Jake placed the box in her hand. She managed to open it with shaky hands. The ring inside took her breath away. There was a round cut sapphire in the center, with a smaller baguette style diamond running along either side of the setting.

The unassuming elegance took her breath away. "Oh, Jake. It's incredible."

"It was my grandmother's. She was a huge fan of Grace Kelly, and when my grandfather was ready to propose, he found as close of a lookalike to Grace's engagement ring as he could. But he knew she loved sapphires more than diamonds, and he knew a jeweler through a friend of a friend who swapped out a diamond for the sapphire. Or at least that's the story he always told."

"He sounds like a man who really knew the woman he loved."

"Pop loved her more than anything in the world. She told me once that nobody else on earth knew her as well as Pop did, not even her best friend Dottie."

Rose cupped Jake's cheek. "Sounds like you learned a thing or two from him."

"Pop made sure I did. Before she passed, she gave the ring to me, and told me to give it to the girl who made me complete. I know you never got a chance to meet her while we were dating, but I told her everything about you. I think she knew I was a lovestruck fool who was going to marry you one day."

Rose thought back to her own grandmother, and the cardinals she'd spotted in the bushes earlier. Maybe two particular souls were more responsible for the freak blizzard than Mother Nature was, after all. "I'm sorry I never met her, she sounds wonderful."

Jake nodded to the ring, still in the box. "May I?"

"Yes, of course."

Rose held out her hand as Jake gently extricated the ring and slipped it on her left hand. "It's even the right size." She kissed him, and whispered, "I love you."

"I love you, too."

Daisy woke up, stretched, and eased her way around the couch to sniff at Rose, and at the ring on her hand. The dog gave it a small lick and then kissed Jake's face, tail wagging the entire time.

Rose's phone buzzed in her pocket. She pulled it out and laughed at the message on the screen. "My apartment has power again."

EPILOGUE

Two Weeks Later

"I had a great time with Megan and Caleb tonight, babe. Thank you for suggesting they come over for dinner."

Rose let Daisy back inside the house, the reflectors on her new pink collar catching the light. Rose knelt and went into the new training routine to clean and dry off Daisy's paws. She told Daisy, "Sit, paw," and held out her hand. Daisy followed each command, the thump of her tail the only sign of her excitement and impatience.

"You're such a good girl," Rose cooed as she worked on each paw and underbelly. It had snowed again two days ago, and Daisy had spent as much time in it as she could. "Good girl. Okay!" Rose gave the release command and Daisy bounded into the kitchen to give Jake a quick wiggle hello and then ran off into the rest of the house.

"She's such a silly dog." Jake laughed. "Tonight was fun. Caleb seems like a good guy, and Megan looks happy." Jake hadn't spent too much time with Megan when they were all teenagers, but Rose knew Jake wanted her family to be as happy as possible.

He'd finished cleaning up the kitchen and leaned against the counter, arms crossed over his chest.

"She is. I'm glad those two figured things out." Rose hung Daisy's towel and joined Jake in the kitchen. He pulled her into an embrace, and Rose snuggled into his chest – the safest place in the world, in his arms.

"They seem excited about their wedding plans."

"Mm," she replied. Rose had enthusiastically agreed to be a bridesmaid for Megan. It was going to be a smallish wedding, with just family members in the bridal party and no extended bonding trips.

Rose looked up at Jake, her neck craned back to see his face. "Is that what you want for our wedding?"

Jake brushed a few strands of hair away from her face. "The actual wedding is less important to me than the marriage. But I do have one thing I'd like to include in whatever we do."

"Oh?" Rose couldn't imagine what it was.

"We'll have whatever size and kind of wedding you want, but I'd like us to find somewhere that we can bring Daisy with us and have her be part of the ceremony."

"Really? I love that idea!"

Jake kissed her, long and deep, and for a moment there was nothing else in the world except his arms around her and their hearts beating in time. He pulled away and pressed his forehead against hers. "I know you don't want a big wedding and have said 'the smaller, the better,' and I want to honor that. How do you feel about eloping?"

"Really? You'd be okay with that?"

"We've already had to deal with a bunch of opinions from everyone in our lives. And no matter how well-intentioned they might be, I know that it's stressing you out. That's unacceptable to me."

Jake wasn't wrong. Rose had skillfully avoided calls from her mother the last three days because she hadn't wanted to deal with the suggestions her mother wanted to make and then demand Rose implement in a wedding that didn't even have a date or location. Not to mention the carefully worded congratulations from Jake's mother and the raised eyebrows and whispers of everyone else in their lives. She knew he'd spoken to everyone he could and told them to back off with the judgment because it was none of their business.

Still, Rose didn't want to be a sour sport about things. She pulled away and stepped out of his arms to grab a drink from the fridge. She passed a bottle to Jake and kept one for herself. "Planning a wedding can be stressful. There's a lot of pieces to the puzzle."

"What if it didn't need to be stressful? What if there were only a handful of pieces to it? You, me, Daisy, an officiant, and a photographer."

It sounded ideal to Rose. "You'd be okay with something that small?"

"Hell yeah. You'd be less stressed out, and at the end of the day I get to call you 'my wife' and make love to you. I'm happy."

"That sounds like the perfect day. Do you have a destination in mind?" Rose opened the bottle from one of the local breweries, Starfire Brews. It was the longest running brewery in the area, and apparently the next generation was in the process of taking it over.

"Not yet, but I have a date in mind." Jake drank from his beer and then grinned at her. "Let's go search for a place." He led the way out of the kitchen to the bedroom where his laptop was currently charging next to the bed.

Rose followed him, confused. "What do you mean you have a date in mind?" She sat on the bed next to him, her legs criss-crossed, beer still in hand. "When is it?"

Jake booted up his laptop. "Do you want to stay on the Island, head upstate, or go out of state?"

Rose persisted, undeterred from his deflection. "Jake. What's the date?"

"This weekend." Jake pulled up some options for bed and breakfasts in the tri-state area and started clicking on links to open the pages.

Rose counted out the dates until the weekend. Saturday was the twenty-first. "Why this weekend?"

"Ah, found one. What do you think of this place?" He turned the laptop so she could better see the screen, and Rose immediately fell in love with the location. The Wild Oak B&B, an 'updated farmhouse with historic charm,' with easy access to antique stores and highly-rated restaurants in the small town of Oakridge, New York.

"It's perfect."

Jake made the call to see if there was a room available, which didn't seem likely the weekend before Christmas. Rose made a list of everything else they needed to do so she didn't go crazy wondering if they'd have a place to get married this weekend.

"You'll never believe it. They had a cancellation this morning and their honeymoon suite was available. It's now ours."

It felt like a sign. "What!? Really? That's – that's amazing."

A handful of hours and phone calls had an officiant and a local photographer reserved for that weekend. Jake had disappeared to organize some things with his job, so Rose pulled out her green hard-shell suitcase. She organized her clothes and lingerie for the weekend, a few newer items she hadn't worn yet tucked neatly into a makeup bag.

It was only when she'd packed everything and put the suitcase by the bedroom door that the realization hit her.

She didn't have a dress.

· · ·

There weren't many options in her closet because she was still unpacking, and the middle of December wasn't prime 'pretty dress' time. Still, she needed something special.

Jake had offered up space in his garage for anything she wanted to take her time to unpack, and that's where she shoved her dress rack. Her previous apartment didn't have much closet space, being a studio above a garage, so the portable dress rack had been a lifesaver.

She picked her way through the smaller stacks of boxes that housed her books and mementos until she found the dresses – all hung in garment bags, per her mother's instruction.

Rose opened the first bag on the rack and found a long flowy summer dress with a bright floral design. No go. The next bag had a blue dress from a coworker's wedding the year before last. It would make a good last resort option.

Panic grew and her chest felt tight as she checked more bags and didn't see anything that felt remotely like it'd be a suitable choice.

She'd started to think that she'd have to go do last minute shopping and settle for something that maybe didn't quite fit or wasn't her style.

Rose tugged another zipper down and checked inside the next bag. A dark blue dress from a wedding a few years ago. But there was something green behind it on the hanger.

She tried to pull the green fabric out of the bag but almost pulled the whole rack down. Rose freed the specific hanger from the mess of them and brought the whole thing to the bedroom. Jake was still out so she didn't have to worry about him finding her choosing a dress, not that they'd be able to avoid the whole superstition about seeing the bride before the ceremony if they were sharing a room the night before.

Rose hung the bag on the closet door and pulled both dresses out and off the hanger. She tossed the blue dress onto the bed, focused instead on the dark green dress she'd completely forgotten existed. She'd worn it to a holiday charity event with her parents a few years ago. The long-sleeve casual dress had a wrap V-neck that showed off her chest in a tasteful way. It fell just above her knees and had pockets.

She stripped out of her leggings and oversized t-shirt and stepped into the dress. It pulled over her hips easily and she was able to get her arms into the sleeves without issue. But the zipper wouldn't cooperate no matter how she contorted herself to reach it.

"I've always thought you look amazing in green."

Rose whirled to find Jake leaning against the doorframe to the bedroom. Daisy hadn't made a peep when he got home, but she waited in the hallway behind Jake. "I didn't know you were home."

"Only just got here, but I didn't mean to startle you. Sorry."

Rose waved it off. "No big deal. I was just, um…"

"Trying on dresses?"

She nodded. "I wanted to see if this one still fits. For Saturday."

Jake stepped into the room until he was in front of Rose, close enough for her to breathe him in. "May I?"

"Please." Rose turned to face away from him and pulled her hair over her shoulder so it wouldn't be in his way. She lifted her gaze and stared at the reflection of them in the full-length mirror hung on the closet door, and their eyes locked. Her breaths came faster as she watched Jake trail his eyes over her reflection.

Jake smirked as he stepped even closer; she could feel his breath on her bare neck. Tingles erupted where Jake's fingers brushed against her waist and then further up her back. He pulled the zipper up without trouble and hooked the small clasp at the top.

The dress fit just as well as the first time she wore it. "What do you think?" She did a small spin before Jake grabbed her by her waist and pulled her in close.

"You look beautiful." Jake placed a small kiss on the bare skin of her neck. "I look forward to marrying you and then taking it off."

The promise in his words made her shiver. She could hardly wait to marry him and knew without a doubt she'd made the right decision.

Still, the stress of moving for the second time in less than a year combined with the judgmental rants Rose got from her mother about the engagement while also shoving opinions about the wedding at her, all right before the holidays, was a little much. She hadn't been sleeping all that well the last few days.

"You know," she looked up at Jake through her lashes. "Eloping really is the perfect idea. I'm so glad you suggested it." She ran her fingers down his back and hooked her thumbs into the waist of his jeans.

Jake kissed her, the back of her head cradled in one of his hands.

"I've always wanted to run away with you, Rose."

She grinned at him. "Then help me get out of this dress so we can do exactly that."

"As you wish," he whispered.

STARFIRE LAKE

<u>Weekend Temptation</u> (Abbie & Derek's story)

<u>Wayward Temptation</u> (Megan and Caleb's story)

Sign up to my <u>newsletter here</u> to keep up-to-date on release information, giveaways, sales, and sneak peeks!

And you can find all of my <u>social media links here</u>. Be sure to give a follow & say hi!

ACKNOWLEDGMENTS

A book is never written in a vacuum and there are always people to thank and credit for the project getting all the way to the "published" stage.

Husband – thank you for being mine, and for loving me as I am. In this life and the next, my love.

Chipmunk – I am the luckiest mama in the world. You are so kind, smart, and funny, and I love that you think mama writing a book is "so cool."

Wifey – I couldn't do this (or life) without you. As a very wise fictional character said, "Family don't end in blood."

Melissa Wolfe – Thank you for being a friend!

Blue Saffire – Look, I did it again!

My writing community – Jeannie Moon, Patty Blount, Zoe York, Carrie Lomax, Stacey Agdern, Jayne Rylon, Eve Pendle, Brighton Walsh, Katie Lillig, Kate Nolan, Lexi Ryan, Tara Wyatt, Sophie Andrews: I couldn't do any of this without you.

Holland Rae – My late-night writing buddy, I don't know what I'd do without your support and help.

Rebecca – Thank you for your help with this book!

Kristina P. – Proofreader extraordinaire, thank you! I'd like to note that any typos or mistakes in this book are my own and probably because I ignored her advice.

Naomi Lane – Thank you for putting up with me changing my mind a bunch of times before the cover was perfect! Give your fur babies kisses from me!

Bellevue Crew – Couldn't do this Mom thing without ya'll.

My family and friends – I love you all so much and appreciate your encouragement and support!

Nyx & Lila – you two are my best buddies, and I love getting to spend the days with you wild pups. Thank you for loving Chipmunk as much as you do and being the best older furry siblings to him. I love you both, and writing wouldn't be the same without your company.

My readers - thank you. I hope you liked the book, but I also know not every book is going to be everyone's cup of tea. It doesn't matter if you're a new-to-me reader or someone who has read one of my other books, thank you for giving this story a chance.

ABOUT THE AUTHOR

Though she grew up on Long Island, Vivi Parish now lives in the suburbs of Texas with her husband, toddler, and two very sweet dogs. You can find Vivi active on social media posting photos of her dogs and daily life.

Be sure to sign up for her newsletter for book updates. You can find her on social media here.

Her website is www.viviparish.com.